TRUCK STOP FANTASY

GAY PUBLIC SEX SERIES #2

NICO FOX

CONTENTS

TRUCK STOP FANTASY

One week after college graduation, I was off to start my new life in Chicago at my dream internship at a prestigious financial firm. I said my goodbyes to family and friends, packed my few meager belongings into the trunk and was off to a new life.

Miles of cornfield surrounded me, and I knew there would be miles to come. That's the price you pay for growing up in Nebraska. Didn't bother me though.

That stretch of Interstate 80 would bring me money, sex, and a new exciting life. I switched the dials on the radio to see if there was anything other than a preacher telling me I was going to hell, but there wasn't, so I popped in my iPhone to keep myself awake. Just as the third Lady Gaga song started, the gas light blinked red.

Shit! Why didn't I stop outside Omaha to fill up? The last road sign said that the nearest truck stop was thirteen miles away.

As the dial dipped below one quarter, then to one tenth, and the red light blinked, my heart sank. If I got stranded, there was nobody for miles that could rescue me.

There wasn't even cell reception. That's how far out in the middle of nowhere I was. And that's coming from me, a guy from western Nebraska.

The next sign said five more miles. If I ran out of gas, I'd have to walk five miles to the gas station and five miles back. Ouch! I slowed my speed to conserve gas and turned off the air-conditioning, not that it made a difference.

Everything on this crappy ten-year-old car was falling apart, including the air-conditioning. It let out some cold air, but not enough to cool the car even after running on full-speed for two hours. Sweat poured off my forehead and my balls itched. Once I got to Chicago, I would ditch this piece of shit.

"Truck Stop: 1 mile." Phew. I wanted to change my under-wear more than anything. I'd been to truck stops before, they're pretty common along the interstate. Some are large complexes, with a car wash, restaurants, clean bathrooms, and showers.

This one was small and run down. I pulled into the gas station to fill up and buy some snacks. There were two semis in line of the weigh station, but the only other person was the man behind the counter reading a magazine. He didn't even look up when I pulled in.

The sun blazed in my eyes and dust blew over the pave-ment. I laughed to myself when it reminded me of a western movie from the Dust Bowl days, where tumble-weeds rolled over and banjos played in the background.

After grabbing some essential snacks and energy drinks, I moved the car to the side where I saw the sign showing free showers. I thought I could grab a quick one before hitting the road again.

In the back of the truck near the park area was the public bathroom. I guzzled one water and went to take a piss. I pulled out my cock at the dingy urinal and relieved myself.

A cool breeze rushed through the bathroom. It felt good to hold my cock in my hands for something other than a quick piss. The last few days had been so hectic, with packing and moving plans, that I hadn't had the chance to rub one out in between.

My dick grew a little, and I tugged twice. It wasn't fully hard, but it was getting there. Outside, a car rustled its way through the gravel nearby.

Just as the last few drops of piss were escaping my slit, the door opened and a thin guy, probably in his mid-thirties walked in. We didn't acknowledge each other, and I couldn't see his treasure as he unzipped in front of the only other urinal in the bathroom.

Small wooden blocks that didn't go above my chest-level, gave a small bit of privacy. The sound of piss on porcelain echoed through the small tiled bathroom and off the cement floors.

I desperately wanted to know if he was thinking about me standing next to him. I stood there with my cock in my hand, standing next to a guy I didn't know and probably would never touch, but it was the closest to intimacy that I'd had in a long time. He zipped up and walked out without washing his hands. The thrill of it got me even harder.

When he left, I fantasized about him looking over at my dick, wanting to touch me, wishing I could glance over at his, too. Poetic, really. The sexual tension just from standing next to this total stranger was enough to satiate my hunger for affection at this time in my life.

As my cock engorged, I massaged the skin. Too bad my favorite lube was buried deep in my packed boxes. Grime covered the corner tiles, stray pubic hairs lay on the cement floor, and the stench of urinal cake made the environment filthy, yet exciting.

It reminded me of the last time I went to Chicago for Pride, and took part in all sorts of sex parties in the basements of bars, things that would never happen in Nebraska. The best we had were Grindr hookups in the cornfield which is sexier than it sounds.

I spit on my cock for lubrication and went at it. Man, I would have given anything for that guy to jerk me off at this moment, but I was alone, and I needed to release before I got back on the road. Just as I got into the rhythm, I heard footsteps in the gravel outside so I stopped.

A tall, hot blonde guy walked in carrying a duffle bag. I turned my head slightly, not enough to make it obvious, but enough to see who it was. My heart jumped as I realized just how incredibly sexy he was, probably another college graduate moving across country to start a new job.

He burst through the door with urgency, but as he stepped up, he proceeded with caution. For a second there, our eyes met, even though we didn't look eye-to-eye.

He must have noticed me checking him out, because he hesitated before stepping up to the urinal next to me. He hung his bag from a coat hook on the wall. I nodded to acknowledge him and turned my head back to face the blue tiles in front of me.

A few droplets of piss fell from my now deflated cock, but for all intents and purposes, my bladder was empty. But I didn't want to move just yet, so I stood there, dick hanging, heart beating.

This guy was tall enough to look down over the wooden dividers and see me. His eyes wandered and so did mine. I could only see the base of his dick where it met his plush pubic hair, but I bet he could see my entire cock.

Then the sound of his full bladder shooting at porcelain brought me back to Earth and he let out a sigh.

"Finally able to relieve myself," he said, giving a little bit of a sneer. I gave one back but couldn't muster out a yeah. "Been driving for hours. Can't wait to grab a shower before hitting the road again." He nodded his head in the other direction.

I had forgotten about my shower and didn't notice the sign for it behind us. I turned my head to look at it. Usually truck stops have clean, private showers for about ten bucks, but this place just had an old ratty shower curtain covering what could have been mistaken for a closet.

His piss slowed down to a trickle, and I turned by head back toward my urinal, taking a quick glance at him shaking the rest out. He did not try to hide the view of his cock.

I had cruised at truck stops in Nebraska before, but out there, I knew where the special spots were. No way chances in a place I'd never been. I didn't want to make a move if I wasn't sure.

"You pee shy?" he asked. He looked down at my cock, getting harder, and obviously not peeing.

"Just getting out the last few drops," I choked out.

"Lemme help you there." He reached around the wooden divider and grabbed my cock and shook it. "Shake it nice and good and get all the piss out," he said.

My cock stiffened, and he rubbed his hand over and over. His hands were rough with callouses, probably from husking corn, or baling hay, or at least it turned me on to imagine it was.

The bathroom door suddenly opened, and an older trucker in a sleeveless white undershirt walked in and saw the blonde guy jerking me off. He shook his head in disgust and went into the stall and peed.

I shooed the blond guy's hand away. Even though we'd already been caught, I didn't want to make it worse.

The man rushed out of the stall and did a quick swipe of hands underneath the water, skipping the soap and dryer, sneering in disapproval as he left the bathroom.

It reminded me of a time that someone caught me with a hook-up in the Walmart parking lot. He was a twink I met in my sophomore year at the state university. We were doing a biology project together and started to fool around in my dorm room.

We couldn't risk getting caught though, so he drove us out to the local Walmart. He parked far from the store, where there were no other cars. He went down on me and I closed my eyes.

Something awakened me from my bliss when I heard a car horn honk outside and a group of frat boys calling us "faggots" and throwing bottles at our car. We high-tailed it out of there, but the rush was worth it. Getting caught was just part of the turn on, but their condemnation made it dirtier and sexier.

"How about that shower?" He grabbed his bag and headed toward the showers behind us. I stuffed my hard cock into my shorts and walked over, not bothering to zip up.

He whipped off his summer sandals and tossed them in the lockers next to the bench. He slowly peeled his shirt off like an onion in the humidity. A light dust of golden chest hair glistened in the fluorescent lights.

"You gonna stand there all day?" I was still at the urinal, dumbfounded. I stuffed my hard cock into my shorts and walked over, not bothering to zip up. "Jason, by the way."

He reached into the shower to turn it on. I grabbed the bottom of my shirt to start to take it off but he stopped me.

"Nope. I'm going to undress you all by myself." A chill went down my spine when he took control. He ran his hand over my chest and I did the same. His pecs were hard as a rock and so were his nipples.

"And your name is?" he asked with a suggestive inflection as if he were waiting for me to say it after he gave me his.

"Oh, I'm Nick. Sorry. Got distracted," I replied.

He teased his boxer briefs down like he was doing a strip show for me. He spun them once on his index finger and threw it into my face. I should have been outraged at the insult, but instead I enjoyed the musk coming from the damp sweat on his underwear.

Their scent filled my lungs before they fell to the floor. I felt the need to smell all of him before he showered the tantalizing aroma away.

Like a magnet, my face lowered to his glorious cock standing straight and curving to the left. I ran my nose up and down the length of his shaft and into his sweat-filled pubic hair.

"Not yet," he teased. He undid the button on my shorts and they fell to the floor. He cupped my balls outside my briefs and then yanked them to the floor as well.

"How come I've never seen you around here? This is the best cruising spot in Iowa," he said.

Damn, I was still in Iowa? I thought I had already crossed the damn Mississippi. It's just one big cornfield until the suburbs of Chicago.

Many hours of lonely driving and then a lonely new life where I know nobody. But for this sliver of time, I have someone, someone to touch, and be touched by.

"I'm from Nebraska," I said as we caressed each other's cocks. "Truck stops in Nebraska have action too. Sometimes I'd hang there to get some action from a lonely truck driver who hadn't seen his wife in weeks. I've never done it in the showers though. Always in the back seat of the semi."

Why was I telling him my life story?

"So, you're not a truck stop virgin, just an Iowa virgin." We both laughed. "I promise to show you a good time."

At that, I kneeled down and took him in my mouth. He moaned in pleasure and thrusted himself into the back of my throat before stopping and pulling out of my mouth, running the bottom of the shaft against my hungry tongue.

"Not so fast," he said in a mocking voice.

"You can store your clothes in my locker." Jason pulled out a padlock and stuffed everything in before locking it.

Our naked, sweaty bodies needed a good cleaning. After running the shower for five minutes, it was steaming up. The bathroom door flung open, and before the next guy could see us both, Jason jumped into the shower to avoid being caught, leaving me stark naked.

This new guy looked like he was in the military with his buzz cut and green Army gear. He did a double take when he saw me standing there naked.

I laughed nervously. "I'm just waiting for the shower." The guy raised his eyebrows and looked me up and down before it even occur to me to cover myself up.

My cock was still semi erect. While peeing, the Army guy kept turning his head to look at me. I didn't know if he was here to cruise or if he would bash my face in.

It was nerve-racking to be so vulnerable in a cruising spot that I wasn't familiar with. Either way, he got an eyeful of my assets.

Jason dropped the soap twice in the shower, each time playfully pointing his ass towards me through the shower curtain. I couldn't help but laugh.

Neither could the Army guy. He zipped up at the urinal but couldn't take his eyes off of me, making it pretty obvious. I rested my arms at my side and let him have a good look. It got my heart racing.

My cock filled up again when I realized he was interested. He must be one of those regulars Jason was talking about.

He went to wash his hands while looking me straight in the eye, but seeming to realize I was filthy, didn't bother.

Each step he took closer to me was more exhilarating than the last. My dick was rock hard by now. He put one hand on my chest and the other grabbed my cock. He looked over my shoulder at the shower and laughed.

"Hey Jason, I had a feeling that that was you in there."

I turned around and looked at Jason's gleaming face. "You two know each other?"

"Hell yeah, we're both regulars. Trevor and I know all the cruising spots in Iowa," Jason said.

"There's more than one?" I asked with a grin.

"Hell yeah," Jason said. "We're much more sophisticated than you rural Nebraskan hay seeds." They both laughed.

Trevor's eyes widened as he put his hands around my tight torso. "Hot damn, I thought you were a yuppie coastie. But I just love it when Nebraska boys come through town."

Jason opened the shower curtain while the water was still running and spilled some water on the floor. "Look how clean I am."

He ran his hands up and down his soapy pecs and washboard abs. "When are you two filthy hillbillies going to get in here and wash up?"

He pulled the padlock key from the soap dish and tossed it at Trevor.

Trevor whipped off his clothes. He was just as built as Jason, but with a slightly furrier chest and a deep tan. Damn, baling hay must be better than PX90.

His cock was larger than Jason's, but not as thick. I couldn't keep my hands off of his purple head. Jason grabbed me by the arm and pulled me into the shower. Not long after, Trevor joined us.

Jason kissed me and captivated me with his powerful tongue. I almost forgot about Trevor until Trevor grabbed my ass cheeks and spread them.

He kneeled down and moved his own tongue around the rim of my hole. Jason pulled my head down toward his cock so I could simultaneously suck him off and spread open wide for Trevor.

It felt so good to be used like this. A single blue vein crossed Jason's pink shaft, and a followed it up and down with the tip of my tongue. I moaned as he stuffed my face.

Trevor entered me with one finger, then two. He pulled tugged my hole ever wider until finally, the head of his cock slinked in. "Open wide," he said. "For both of us."

The shower was running over our heads, and bits of water trickled in my mouth between slurps. The door of the bathroom opened, but I'm not sure how many people came in because the shower curtain blocked my view.

I wanted someone to come over and catch me in this compromising pose, bent over and stuffed at both ends. I wanted to be humiliated.

"Don't move until they leave," Jason said in my ear. "We don't know who that is and don't want to get in trouble." I could only murmur a yes before Jason pulled his dick out of my mouth.

When Trevor tried to pull out of me, my ass muscles suctioned hard and wouldn't let him go. We stayed still there for a minute. When we heard a flush and a closing of the bathroom door again, they resumed fucking both ends without warning.

Trevor and Jason worked out a rhythm, in which Trevor would thrust into my ass pushing my mouth forward onto Jason's cock.

They worked in tandem and I was just the drum they were beating. Just their instrument in the orchestra.

I had to brace myself with both hands on the shower wall and was desperate to touch myself. With each lunge, Trevor hit my prostate, bringing me closer and closer to orgasm. I'd never orgasmed without someone touching my dick.

Jason's cock quivered in my mouth as his moans got louder and louder. Soon, he was fucking my face faster than Trevor fucked my ass and he couldn't hold it in any longer. His cream coated the back of my throat and I licked whatever I could from that position.

"Come on, Trevor. Fuck him hard," Jason said. They started making out while I was still bent over, Jason's cock still in my mouth. Trevor plunged into me until he shot his load. They put their faces together, nose-to-nose as they caught their breath and gave each other the occasional kiss.

Just as soon as Trevor pulled out his cock, he re-inserted his finger. I wasn't sure what he was doing, so I started to stand up. Jason gave me a warning. "Not yet. It's your turn." It's obvious that Jason and Trevor had worked this angle before.

Trevor throttled my prostate like he owned it. Jason's cock hung there in my mouth, fat and still half swollen. He had already nourished me with his semen, but this was a new kind of pleasure.

A wave of bliss emanated from my prostate and then through the rest of my body and exploding out of my cock. My whole body erupted in orgasm.

Jason slipped his cock out of my mouth. My jaw was sore, but satisfied.

"How do you like that for humiliation?" Jason asked. I shook my head yes before he soaped us all up. He stepped out to get dressed and Trevor soon followed.

I continued to wash the come off of my stomach and soak myself all around, while they got their clothes out of the locker. They became quiet, and I heard the door open.

I figured another guy had come into the bathroom and they cooled down the flirty banter. I turned off the shower and wiped off excess water. When I opened the shower curtain, they were gone.

They left a small towel for me to dry off. That's how it is with hookups. Come and go. At least I had a good time and would have a good story to tell people about my trip through Iowa.

I turned to the locker to get my stuff and realized my clothes weren't there. Panic hit my chest as I struggled to breathe. Sure, I had more clothes in the car, but my car keys and wallet were in my shorts pocket.

How was I going to get into my car? I walked around the bathroom hoping that I would find my clothes under the bench or around the corner or near the sink. They were nowhere to be found.

My heart beat so fast it almost popped out of my chest. I opened the door a tad bit to look out. There were no cars, no people, nothing. I covered my junk and walked out toward my car.

Of course I always lock it. I was hoping to pry open the door but no luck. Remembering the power window function on the passenger side broke down last year, I tried to pull it down with force.

No luck there either. Panicked, I ran around the car, trying to open anything I could. I would have to walk into the gas station, buck naked, and ask the guy behind the counter to help me open the car. And it would all be caught on camera.

My heart sank when I imagined it making the local news with just my bits covered to make the censors. How humiliating.

Just as I walked toward the gas station, Jason called my name from behind the bushes while waving my t-shirt in the air. Him and Trevor stood up trying to contain their laughter.

"Just playing a trick on you, dude. A bit of Iowa hospitality." Jason and Trevor laughed while patting me on the back. "No hard feelings?"

Jason looked in my eyes as if begging for forgiveness.

Now that I realized they didn't actually leave with my clothes and car keys, it was kind of funny and sexy. A little bit of humiliation got my adrenaline going too.

Walking out into the hot Midwestern summer air completely naked was freeing in a way that I had never experienced before.

In Nebraska, I'd been in group orgies and had run naked through cornfields toward the end of harvest season. But you're still hidden by the corn stalks.

I wouldn't be worried about being seen as much as I was propelling my balls into the corn husk. Quite painful, I know from experience. All part of living as a gay man in Nebraska. They probably do the same thing in Iowa.

Jason and Trevor tossed my clothes back and forth between them like they were playing catch with a ball.

"Come and get 'em." Jason called out. I walked towards them. "No, no," Jason said. "Hands at your side. No covering."

I did as he said, leaving myself in full view of drivers on the interstate. Too bad there wasn't anybody else around.

When I got to the bushes, Trevor gave me my clothes, and I put them on. "Maybe next time you're driving through Iowa, you can stop to see me," Trevor said.

"I'll stop to see both of you."

Jason shook his head no. "I'm from here, but live in Chicago now. Just visiting family, and of course, the truck stop." He laughed when I didn't respond. "What? Are you shocked that I don't bale hay for a living?"

"No, it's just that I'm on my way to Chicago too. I'm starting an internship for Joyce Financials."

Trevor and Jason erupted in laughter. "What a coincidence," Jason said. "I'm the Internship Coordinator for Joyce Financials. Guess I'll be seeing more of you."

ABOUT THE AUTHOR

Hi, I'm Nico. I love to write gay stories about public sex, cruising, bathhouses, anything taboo and a little bit dirty.

When I'm not writing, I love hanging out at the bars and binge-watching Netflix alike.

If you enjoyed this book, sign up for the Mailing List and receive a FREE book.

See you next time

-Nico

Join the Mailing List

For more information:
www.NicoFoxAuthor.com

ALSO BY NICO FOX

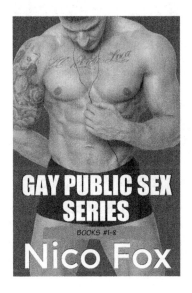

The complete Gay Public Sex Series box set. **Eight** steamy
M/M erotic stories full of **public** encounters.

This bundle includes:

Bulge on a Train

Truck Stop Fantasy

Fitting Room Temptation

Ferris Wheel Threesome

Hole in the Wall Exhibitionist

Ride-Share Stripper

Gay Resort Weekend

Art Gallery Awakening

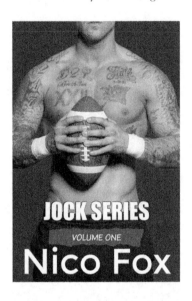

The first Jock Series box set. **Six** steamy M/M erotic stories full of **sweaty athletic guys**.

This bundle includes:

Captain of the Swim Team

First Time, First Down

Soccer Jockstrap

Slammed By the Team

Team Catcher

Heavyweight Punch

The first DILF Series box set. Six stories about
hot daddies and their younger counterparts.

This bundle includes:

DILF of My Dreams

Seduced by the DILF

My Boss is a DILF

First Time Gay with My Girlfriend's Dad

My Girlfriend's Dad Wants It

First Time Gay with the DILF Professor

CRUSH ON MY
STRAIGHT BEST
FRIEND
Nico Fox

*"I always follow his lead about anything and everything. All of our friends
do. He uses his charm and imposing stature to convince us to do anything he
wants."*

Finn always had a crush on his best friend, Cameron, who is *very*
popular with the girls. Standing next to well-built, captain of the
football team, and all-around stud Cameron makes Finn feel a
little, shall we say, less than…insecure.

Cameron has always protected Finn from others when they make
fun of him for his small stature and he's always felt secure
with him.

Finn invites Cameron over for a night of video games and beer
only to be shocked when Cameron makes a wager on a game
that Finn can't say no to. Who says fantasies don't come true?

Dustin has landed his dream job in Silicon Valley just one month after graduating college. He tries to keep his head down as much as he can, despite being surrounded by **hyper-masculine alphas** that call each other *bro.* He just can't stop lusting after the company's founder, notorious womanizer and billionaire's son, Brett.

The company is in peril. A bug in their software may cause one of their biggest customers to leave them. Everyone in the office is nervous, but they try to cover it up with heavy drinking after work and carrying on with their secret Santa ritual.

But Dustin solves the bug, making him the company hero. Brett is eternally grateful to his new employee for saving his company. Find out how this straight stud will pay back his employee in this new erotic story from Nico Fox.

Angels and Devils

Nico Fox

A SEXY underground Halloween party…

*"It's amazing how far two people in love will go to hide their inner desires
from each other."*

Lucas is a shy college student. His boyfriend, Colton, is an
extroverted sports stud that every guy on campus wants to get
with. Together, they have the perfect relationship. Or so it seems.

Lucas is worried someone will steal Colton away because he's
such a catch. What's more, Lucas doesn't know if he can trust
himself to handle monogamy.

They head into Manhattan to look for the perfect Halloween
costumes for their upcoming school party. They want sexy
costumes to show off all that hard work in the gym.

At the costume store, they meet Ace, a sophisticated New Yorker
throwing his own Halloween party, one where inhibitions are
thrown to the wind.

Ace seems a little shady. The party is so elusive that they need to be blindfolded as they ride in a limo to the party. But that's the price Lucas is willing to pay to go to a real New York City party.

How will Lucas and Colton's relationship hold up after a wild night at the party? Will jealousy get in the way, or will exploration bring their relationship to new heights?